STATISTICS AND DATA COMPREHENSION

DATA GEEK

JO ANGELA OEHRLI

Published in the United States of America by Cherry Lake Publishing
Ann Arbor, Michigan
www.cherrylakepublishing.com

Series Adviser: Kristin Fontichiaro

Photo Credits: Cover and page 1, ©Phongphan/Shutterstock; page 5, ©Aspen Photo/Shutterstock; page 6, ©bikeriderlondon/ Shutterstock; page 7, ©Bosnian/Shutterstock; page 8, stux/Pixabay/Public Domain; page 11, ©Nolte Lourens/Shutterstock; page 12, geralt/Pixabay/Public Domain; page 14, ©Eric Isselee/Shutterstock; pages 18 and 20, ©Rawpixel.com/Shutterstock; page 19, ©Studio Romantic/Shutterstock; page 23, ©Dmytro Vietrov/Shutterstock; page 25, ©Senohrabek/Shutterstock; page 26, ©Solis Images/Shutterstock; page 27, ©Iakov Filimonov/Shutterstock

Library of Congress Cataloging-in-Publication Data has been filed and is available at catalog.loc.gov

Cherry Lake Publishing would like to acknowledge the work of the Partnership for 21st Century Learning.
Please visit *www.p21.org* for more information.

Printed in the United States of America
Corporate Graphics

ABOUT THE AUTHOR

Jo Angela Oehrli is a former high school and middle school teacher who helps students find information on a wide range of topics as a librarian at the University of Michigan Libraries. In 2017, she won the American Library Association's Library Instruction Round Table's Librarian Recognition Award.

TABLE OF CONTENTS

CHAPTER 1
Thinking About Statistics and Math 4

CHAPTER 2
Understanding the Basics................... 10

CHAPTER 3
Thinking About Statistics 17

CHAPTER 4
Comparing and Using Statistics 24

FOR MORE INFORMATION..31
GLOSSARY 32
INDEX.. 32

Thinking About Statistics and Math

You have probably heard the terms **statistics** and **data**. But what do they mean? Data is simply bits of information, often numbers. Each piece of data is known as a data point. Statistics are specific numbers calculated from collections of data. For example, a player's batting average (a statistic) is calculated by dividing his number of hits by the total number of times he went up to bat. Similarly, each home run is one data point. The corresponding statistic is the total sum of home runs in the season or in a player's career.

Making sense of data and statistics can be confusing at first. You might feel like you are looking at a sea of numbers. But we can learn to read and understand those numbers as well as we read words.

If you follow sports, you probably already know something about statistics.

Coaches rely on statistics to figure out which players are best at different things or in different situations.

The information you learn by studying statistics can be used in many ways. It can be used to rank things. For example, let's say you're one of the coaches on a baseball team. Maybe you want to place the players on your baseball team in order based on how many times they got on base during the season. It can also be used to predict a result. If you know your baseball team's win/loss record against a certain team, you can predict how likely it is that you will win the next game against them.

Statistics are a great way to win people over in an argument. Perhaps the manager of your baseball team wants to add a new

Math is a part of statistics, but there are also other things to consider.

player. To convince the owner it is a good idea, the manager might show off the new player's pitching statistics.

Data **comprehension** is about more than just using math to get answers. When we complete a math problem, it is easy to think, "Two plus two is four. I have the answer. Now I'm done!" With statistics, we have to think more carefully about what each number means. What are the two things we are adding to another two things? Why are we adding them together? Things that might not matter in a simple math problem can be very important when dealing with statistics. We also have to wonder

If you read newspapers, you will probably see a lot of statistics. They are especially common in the business and sports sections. Why do you think this is?

where the information came from. We have to ask ourselves why it was collected and how it will be used.

Creating, reading, and understanding statistics are among the many ways that we state arguments, make predictions, and build awareness of what is happening in our world. This book will help you understand the meaning of statistics and the ways you should think about them. You will find that there are general "rules of thumb," or procedures you should follow, when you see statistics. You will learn about good places to find statistics and discover how to understand statistics that you see every day.

Statistics and the World Around Us

Statistics are everywhere. So where can we go to find statistics that are reliable and **accurate**? Government Web sites like those run by the U.S. Census Bureau or the Bureau of Labor Statistics are frequently used in the real world to learn more about who lives in the United States, where they live, and where they work.

Another great source is Statista.com. This site serves up statistics about everything from hockey and hamburger buns to smartphones and Sweden. Visit Statista.com and search for three sets of statistics that affect your life right now. Why are those statistics or topics important to you? What did you learn about the topics from reading the statistics?

CHAPTER 2

Understanding the Basics

Here are a few interesting statistics you might not know.

- The average height of an adult man in the United States is 69.3 inches (176 centimeters).

- 6.5 percent of students in the United States drop out of high school.

- Only about 1 in every 10 Americans eats the recommended amount of fruits and vegetables for a healthy diet.

Other types of statistics are so commonly quoted that they have become part of our everyday language.

- "Four out of five dentists recommend using [a certain type of toothpaste]."

- "It's the most watched comedy on television."

Statistics can help explain whether someone is below or above average height.

Advertisers often use statistics to persuade you to use their products. But what do these statistics really mean?

- "The richest 1 percent of the world's population has as much wealth as the other 99 percent combined."

Before we can really know what these statistics mean, we need to understand the vocabulary people use to describe data. There are a lot of statistical terms out there. Knowing what these words mean will help you figure out the significance of the statistics being described.

Words like *out of, percent* (or the % symbol), and *in every* are signals that a statistic uses a **ratio**. Ratios are used to compare a part of something to the entire thing.

Variables are characteristics that explain exactly what a statistic is measuring. For example, we stated earlier that the average height of an adult man in the United States is 69.3 inches (176 cm). That sentence doesn't say that all people are that height. There are some specific ways in which we're narrowing that down from all people. Words like "United States," "adult," and "men" tell us which variables are in play. This means we can't assume that men living in China are an average of 69.3 inches (176 cm) tall. The sentence clearly states that we are looking only at people from the United States. We can't assume that children or women are that tall, either. The statistic specifies that we are talking about adult men. Knowing the variables in a statistic allows us to know when we can make fair comparisons with other statistics. Only

Rule of Thumb

If you know the language people use to describe statistics, you will have a deeper understanding of what the statistics really mean.

In this group of dogs, the mean, median, and mode height would all give you slightly different results.

one variable can be compared at a time. For example, we might compare this example against the average height of adult men in a different country. Or we could compare it against the average height of an adult woman in the United States.

The word *average* gets used a lot in statistics. An average is meant to explain what the most common measurement or result is in a range of data. In general, when you see the word *average*, it should signal to you that you are about to be told that something is typical. You should be ready to question whether it is fair to use that statistic as a true representation of what is common. You will learn later in the book how to figure out if it is reasonable to identify a statistic as average.

Remember our average adult American man? We know that "average" refers to something that is the most common. However, there are three ways to figure out an average.

- **Mean:** When most people think of "average," they are really thinking of the mean. To calculate a mean, you have to add up all the numbers being measured. Then you divide that result by the total number of things you added together. In the height example, you would add together the heights of a certain number of adult men. Then you would divide that number by the number of men.

- **Median:** When someone uses the median to figure out an average, they start by organizing all the numbers in their data from lowest to highest. They then look through the list and find the number that is right in the middle. If there are two middle numbers, they find the mean of those two numbers.

- **Mode:** The mode is simply the number that appears most often in a list of numbers. If no number is listed at least twice, there is no mode.

Depending on the data you are using, each one of these methods might give you very different results. For example, the median income in the United States is about $50,000. However, because a few people (such as millionaires and billionaires) make far more money than that, the mean income measures about $70,000. When you have extreme **outlier** data, like a rare billionaire among a million or more Americans who make less, the median is generally the better option.

Which of these three methods is best? It depends on the situation. It all depends on what you are measuring and what you want to say about the data. The most important thing to remember is that you need to know which method was used. Then you can determine what effect it might have had on the results. You can also figure out whether the statistic can fairly be compared to other averages.

CHAPTER 3

Thinking About Statistics

Now that we understand some statistical vocabulary, let's use that language to apply statistical thinking to the numbers we find.

Think back again to the statistic about the average height of an adult man in the United States. We are aware of a few details about this number because of the variables in the statistic. But one variable is not being considered precisely: age. There are many ways to consider whether someone is an adult. When someone calculated the average height, did they include men from the age of 16 to senior citizenship? From the age of 18 and up? 21 and up?

Even if all Americans agreed that adulthood begins at a certain age, this number might be different in other cultures. Our statistic about average height in America comes from the Centers

Age is an important variable when considering statistics about peoples' size and other characteristics.

for Disease Control and Prevention (a government agency that is known for having reliable data). This organization defines an adult man in this situation as anyone 20 years of age and older. If you compared the height of American men to the height of men in another country, you would want to be sure that "adult" was defined the same way. Perhaps another country's study includes everyone over 14. This would make it unfair to compare the average heights of the two studies.

If the source of your statistic doesn't give you important information about the variables being used, you might have to do

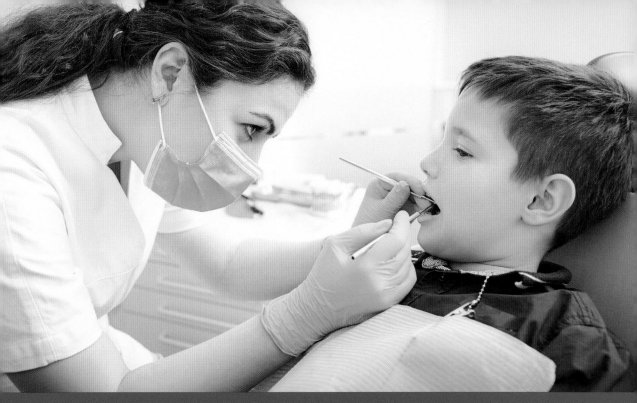

When you hear an advertisement saying that "4 out of 5 dentists recommend" something, ask yourself which dentists were surveyed and whether that's a ratio or the actual number of dentists.

a little research on your own. Google the statistics you find. Do you see the same numbers used on trusted Web sites? Do these sites link the data to another reliable source? Find out exactly what was used to define that number.

Sometimes we can be misled by a statistic because we don't know how a number was figured out. For example, we might not know how many things were counted.

Let's look at the example of four out of five dentists recommending that you use a certain type of toothpaste. What if this number was used because the person collecting this

People involved in advertising and marketing might create statistics that are designed to influence your shopping decisions.

information literally only asked five dentists? (Often, "four out of five" is said to represent a fraction, so it could also be 40 out of 50 or 80 out of 100. We don't know!) Maybe four out of five dentists is enough for you. But what if it were 400 out of 500 dentists or 4 million out of 5 million dentists? The total number of dentists surveyed is called a sample size. Generally, a larger sample size produces more trustworthy data. It can also affect the data's meaning. Consider that, in the last situation, there are 1 million dentists who recommend a different kind of toothpaste. That's a lot of dentists! And what if these dentists were from different countries where this particular brand of toothpaste wasn't available? How would that influence your toothpaste purchase?

There is not always a specific rule about what the numbers representing the parts and the whole of your ratio should be. However, knowing what they are provides important information about whether you can trust a statistic.

Any time you use information, whether it's statistics or any other kind of data, you should investigate the background of its source. Ask yourself these questions:

- **Who** gathered and calculated this statistic? Is it a person or organization you can trust? Do they have a history of providing reliable data? Do they have any reason not to tell the truth? Who supported or funded the gathering of this statistic? Could this have had an influence on the results?

- **What** is being measured or counted? What information is included with this statistic? What information isn't included?

- **Where** does the statistic come from? Are there links or **citations** that lead you to the statistic's original source?

- **When** was this statistic collected? Is it up-to-date?

- **Why** would you use this statistic and not some other data? Why was this data collected? Is it fair to use this statistic for your purpose?

- **How** was this statistic gathered? Is that process described somewhere?

Knowing the answers to some or all of these questions will help you understand a statistic. This will help you figure out how you can use it in your homework or conversations.

Analyzing TV

If you read that a television show was the most watched comedy on TV, how would you determine if this statistic is true? Consider asking yourself these questions.

- *Who figured out that it was the most watched comedy on television? Does this person or organization have anything to gain by making the show seem popular? Even if the show's creators figured out the data, it doesn't necessarily mean it is wrong. However, you should try to understand how they came to their conclusion. Are they trying to get advertisers to give them more money for ads sold during the show's broadcast?*
- *How did they figure out who watched the comedy? Did they count people who watched it online? What if someone watched it twice? Does that count?*
- *Are there **impartial** organizations that can confirm the numbers?*
- *Is this information from this year? Last year? What is the time frame? Maybe the show was really good last year, but it lost an important actor. It might not be as popular as it once was.*

Know what is being counted and how the statistic was calculated.

CHAPTER 4

Comparing and Using Statistics

Comparing one statistic to another is a powerful way of using data to prove a point. However, as we have learned, you can't just compare any two statistics. The more variables differ between two statistics, the less fair it is to compare them. It is also wrong to compare a true statistic against one with false or misleading information.

Is This Number Possible?

Let's go back to the commercial about dentists and think about it in a different way. What if the ad said, "Four million out of five million dentists recommend Toothpaste A?" Before you run out and buy a new tube, ask yourself if this claim even makes sense. Are there even 5 million dentists in the world? That would

Knowing how many people are on Earth will help you understand the significance of statistics about the global population.

be a lot of dentists! According to Worldmapper, there were only 1.8 million dentists working in the world in 2004 (*www .worldmapper.org/display.php?selected=218*). Whenever you see a huge number like that, consider whether it could really be that big.

Is There an Existing Number I Can Compare This To?

As you are reading statistics, you should also compare them to **benchmarks**. Benchmark statistics are commonly known facts

Having a rough idea of how many dentists are in the world will help you determine whether our example statistic was reasonable.

about the world. They are easy to verify with trusted sources. Keep these benchmark statistics in mind as you read and research. When you encounter new information, you can often compare it to these statistical benchmarks. It's a quick way to make sense of new data! Here are some examples:

- There are about 7 billion people in the world.
- There are about 325 million people in the United States.
- About 70 percent of Earth's surface is covered with water.

Sometimes people might collect data by going door to door and asking people questions. If you try this technique, ask an adult to go with you.

Gathering Data

How would you gather data and present statistics at your school? What would you want to know? How would you keep people's information private?

You should learn benchmark statistics about your own community. How many people live in your city or town? How many people live in your state? What is the ratio between how many people live in your town and how many live in your state? Or in your country? Or in the world? Did you know that there are about 6 million babies born in the United States each year? That means there are about 6 million kindergartners, 6 million eighth graders, and 6 million high school seniors in the country at any point. This could be useful information to know if you are reading statistics about U.S. students.

Do Statistics Mean All People Do the Same Thing?

Let's say your family eats breakfast and dinner together at home every day, and you bring a sack lunch to school. It's the same way for your friends: They bring their lunch and eat their other meals at home. If you see a statistic that says that in 2012, 43.1 percent of the nation's food spending was on food prepared away from home (like at a restaurant or café), it might seem impossible. Everyone in your neighborhood does what you do! If you have verified that the data is accurate, just keep in mind that some statistics measure averages. This means your family's zero percent spent eating out is balancing against another family who eats out almost every meal. Getting used to these inconsistencies can take time and practice.

Can I Use Statistics to Predict the Future?

Using statistics to predict the future can be tricky. It is very difficult to prove that one situation from the past will automatically occur again in the future. Think about the food spending example above. We might think that we spend about the same amount of money eating out year after year, so we might "predict" similar behavior from year to year. But what if in the next year the local factory closes and fewer families can afford to eat out? Or a new grocery store opens in town, and now people can walk for groceries instead of having to take the bus? Or there is a big blizzard, and everyone huddles at home for a week? Any or all of those situations could change the statistic. All kinds of variables could pop up that would change people's food budgets.

Conclusion

It can be difficult to think critically about statistics. It can also be tempting to question every statistic you encounter until you don't believe anything you see! But if you simply keep practicing, you'll soon start to see that statistics can be a lot of fun! Every time you see these kinds of data, ask yourself questions such as,

"Where did this number come from?" and "How does it compare to what I already know?" Soon, reading statistics will be second nature. You will know exactly which questions to ask. Statistics will never seem confusing again!

2016 Presidential Election

The results of the 2016 U.S. presidential election came as a huge surprise even to political experts. Before the election, most polls and surveys showed that Hillary Clinton was likely to win. However, Donald Trump won in a surprising upset. After the election, many people tried to figure out why the predictions were so inaccurate.

One of the reasons involved a comparison to past behavior. It was predicted that areas of the country that had voted for President Barack Obama in 2012 would vote for Clinton in 2016. When you see statistics used in this way, you should always ask yourself if people will really act in the same way again. Why or why not? Ask the people around you what they think and why.

For More Information

BOOKS

Colby, Jennifer. *Data in Arguments*. Ann Arbor, MI: Cherry Lake Publishing, 2018.

Oehrli, Jo Angela. *Ethical Data Use*. Ann Arbor, MI: Cherry Lake Publishing, 2018.

WEB SITES

American FactFinder
https://factfinder.census.gov/faces/nav/jsf/pages/index.xhtml
This tool from the U.S. Census Bureau is a great source of interesting statistics about people who live in the United States.

United States Census Bureau: State Facts for Students
www.census.gov/schools/facts
Check out some interesting statistics about the 50 states.

GLOSSARY

accurate (AK-yuh-rit) correct in details

benchmarks (BENCH-marks) known measurements used in comparisons

citations (sye-TAY-shuhnz) credits given to someone else's work

comprehension (kahm-pri-HEN-shuhn) understanding of something

data (DAY-tuh) information, often in number form

impartial (im-PAHR-shuhl) having no reason to treat one side unfairly

outlier (OWT-lye-ur) a data point that is much smaller or larger than the majority of other data points and can therefore affect the mean

ratio (RAY-shee-oh) a comparison of two numbers where one is a whole and the other is a part of that whole

statistics (stuh-TIS-tiks) calculations based on a set of data

variables (VAIR-ee-uh-buhlz) things that can change

INDEX

arguments, 6–7, 8
averages, 4, 10, 13, 14–16, 17–18, 28–29

batting averages, 4
benchmarks, 25–26, 28

Centers for Disease Control and Prevention, 17–18
Clinton, Hillary, 30

elections, 30

food budgets, 28–29

Google, 19
government, 9, 17–18

height, 10, 13, 14, 15, 17–18

income, 16
inconsistencies, 28–29

language, 13

mean, 15
median, 15, 16
mode, 15

Obama, Barack, 30
outliers, 16

percentages, 10, 12, 26, 28–29
polls, 30
predictions, 6, 29, 30

questions, 21–22, 29–30

rankings, 6

ratios, 12, 21
recommendations, 19–21, 24–25
research, 18–19

sample size, 20
sources, 7–8, 9, 18–19, 21–22, 26, 29–30
Statista.com, 9

television ratings, 22
toothpaste, 19–21, 24–25
topics, 9
Trump, Donald, 30

variables, 13–14, 17, 18–19, 24, 29

Web sites, 9, 19, 25
Worldmapper.org, 25